STEPHANIDES BROTHERS'

GREEK MYTHOLOGY

SERIES B: GODS AND MEN   No. 11

DAEDALUS AND ICARUS

retold by MENELAOS STEPHANIDES
illustrated by YANNIS STEPHANIDES

translation BRUCE WALTER

DAEDALUS AND ICARUS

Printed in Greece

1st edition 1982
2nd edition 1986
3rd edition 1987
4th edition 1989
5th edition revised 1991

ISSN 1105-249X
ISBN 960-425-025-6

THE GODS OF THE WINDS

In the old days, whenever the frozen north wind blew in savage blasts, people would say that once again some mortal had enraged Boreas, the mighty winged god who lived in a tall, white castle in the mountains of Thrace.

BOREAS

The castle of Boreas was fair and stately, and the god spent most of his time there. But if ever he got into a rage, he would launch himself from his snowy palace and with great beats of his powerful wings swoop down on the houses of men, bringing frosts, tempests and snowstorms as he came.

Yet Boreas was not always savage and wild: he could also be calm and patient.

He showed how great his patience was when Erechtheus, king of Athens, promised that he would give the god his lovely daughter Oreithyia as a wife. To tell the truth, Erechtheus did not make this promise willingly, for he had no desire to marry off the youngest of his four daughters. He had already found husbands for the other three, but he wished to keep Oreithyia at his side.

Erechtheus let no man set eyes on the beautiful girl. He would not even allow her out of the palace. From the window of her chamber, Oreithyia could see only the sky and nothing more. And so it seemed certain that she would never marry and would never leave her father, whom for all his harshness, she loved dearly.

BOREAS AND OREITHYIA

But one summer day, when Oreithyia opened her window to let in some fresh air, a gentle little north wind caressed her face and ruffled her golden hair. She breathed in its freshness and smiled up at the cloudless sky, her face radiant with beauty.

At that moment Boreas flew past the open window and caught sight of the lovely princess. The winged god fell in love with her on the spot, and without wasting a moment he hastened to her father and begged to let him marry her and take her back to his snowy palace.

It is difficult for a mortal to refuse his daughter's hand to a god, even if that mortal happens to be a king. And it was a thousand times more difficult to refuse Boreas. For no one could resist the fury of the god who commanded the most violent of winds, and disaster could strike the palace of the king if he dared say no.

And so Erechtheus was afraid to deny the winged god. Yet on the other hand, he had no wish to give away his daughter. Finally, pretending to be both pleased and flattered, he said:

"I give you my daughter gladly, Boreas, and I am moved by the honour you have shown me. However, I would like a little time to get her used to the idea, for she has become so accustomed to living alone with her parents that I don't know how she will receive your offer."

"I am delighted to see you are so willing," replied the god. "And much as I would like to take the princess with me now, I shall give you the time that you need. I shall come back for her one month from today."

As soon as the month was up, Boreas returned.

"All is well," Erechtheus told him. "I have persuaded her. But she would like a little time to prepare herself — not leave home just like that. You know what I mean."

ERECHTHEUS PLAYS FOR TIME

In fact, Boreas did not quite know what the king meant. But he decided to be patient for another month and left empty-handed.

When he came back again, Erechtheus said:

"Everything is ready. I have prepared her for her departure. You can take her with you immediately. Only, her mother is ill, and Oreithyia would be very upset if she had to leave with her in this state. You do see my point, don't you?"

Boreas did not see the king's point at all, and suspected that something was amiss. But he pretended to agree, and left yet again without Oreithyia.

When Erechtheus saw how easy-going Boreas was, he became more confident — or, rather, over-confident, and when the god returned once more the king of Athens told him:

"Look, we've talked it all over, we've agreed, nothing stands in the way and as I've told you before, I consider it a great personal honour that you're taking my daughter as your wife. But I've been thinking things over and I'd like to tell you something for your own good. To tell you the truth, I think you're taking a girl who's rather too young. Wouldn't you do better to wait

till she's grown up a little, and is more fit to be your wife and helpmate, and a real mother to your children? Come back in a year or two, and we'll talk it over. Don't tell me that you'll find some other girl in the meantime and forget our little Oreithyia, eh?" And emboldened by his own words, Erechtheus gave Boreas a hearty slap on the back, laughing cunningly to himself.

By now, Boreas saw everything. It was as clear as daylight! Erechtheus didn't want to give away his daughter at all, and each of his requests for delay had been sheer trickery. Yet in spite of his terrible fury, the god of the north wind held himself in check and allowed none of his feelings to show.

"Very well, I shall think it over," he replied, and departed.

He soared high into the clouds, his spirits in a turmoil of rage. Erechtheus had insulted him beyond endurance and the thought of losing Oreithyia was not to be borne.

"What does Erechtheus take me for?" Boreas growled. "It's my own fault for sitting and listening to his excuses for so long; I, who can raise such winds from the north that they tear up hundred-year-old oaks by the roots and flatten lofty cypresses! I, who can whip the ocean waves into towering mountains and lash the earth with hail at will, bringing snow and frost, and freezing water as hard as stone! I, whose wrath men tremble at, to be humbled by Erechtheus and sit there weakly begging his favours like some poor, common mortal! No! I, and I alone, shall decide! I shall take Oreithyia by force and make her my wife!"

With these words he gave a mighty beat of his great wings, and in an

instant a fearsome storm broke upon the earth. The north wind howled wildly, wreaking havoc in its path. With one terrifying blast it struck the palace of Erechtheus, hurling all its doors wide open, and in with it came the winged god, a force no man could resist. Snatching up Oreithyia in his strong arms, he soared off with her high into the heavens.

Soon, the wind dropped and to the earth there came the calm which follows a storm. The anger of Boreas softened into love and the mighty god held his precious burden in a tender embrace as he flew joyfully towards Thrace.

Boreas held a great wedding feast and Oreithyia became mistress of the snowy palace of the mightiest of the gods of the wind. She gave her husband two sons who became fine young men, winged like their father. Their names were Zetes and Calais and they took part in the expedition of the Argonauts, performing many great feats.

Boreas' brothers were the other great winds of the earth: the South wind which brought life-giving rain; Zephyrus, who blew cool and gentle from the West and was loved by all men, and Eurus, a soft and refreshing wind from the East.

The ruler of all these winds was Aeolus.

Aeolus lived happily with his wife, his six sons and his six daughters in an imposing palace on an island off the coast of Italy. In those days it was named Aeolia, but today men call it Stromboli.

Whenever he wished, Aeolus could forbid the winds to blow, and then peace reigned over the whole earth.

AEOLUS AND ODYSSEUS

Long ago, when the war against Troy was coming to its end and the Greeks were returning to their homeland, the waves brought Odysseus, king of Ithaca, to the coast of Aeolia. Poseidon, the mighty ruler of the oceans, had cast the hero's ships onto the shore in his rage when he learned that Odysseus had blinded his son, the fearsome Cyclops, Polyphemus.

Aeolus welcomed Odysseus and his companions to his island. He ordered his six sons to help him repair their ships, and every evening they all gathered in his palace to eat, drink and make merry.

When the god of the winds heard of the misfortunes Odysseus had suffered in his wanderings, he took pity on him and decided to help him return to his native land without further misadventure.

When the time came for their ships to sail, Aeolus thought of a way to protect the mariners from the wrath of Poseidon. He went and slaughtered a large ox and made a bag from its hide; then he captured all the winds except Zephyrus, shut them up inside the bag, and tied it securely with a silver cord in case it came open and let the winds out.

"I am entrusting this to you," Aeolus told Odysseus. "Keep it on board, guard it well, and if you do not open it, you will be in Ithaca within ten days."

When they set sail, Odysseus forbade his companions to touch the bag, and Zephyrus swelled their sails and drove the ships swiftly eastwards towards Greece.

They made good speed for nine days, but on the tenth, when the ships were already nearing Ithaca, and Odysseus was asleep, his companions began to suspect that their leader was keeping something hidden from them.

"He's got treasure in that sack," said one.

"And that's why he's afraid we'll open it," added another.

"We've all fought and suffered together," protested a third, "and now he's hoarding a sack of gold and silver, while we're going home empty-handed."

"Let's open it," urged the first sailor.

"Yes, come on, open it!" they all shouted.

And open it they did.

So, when the mountains of Ithaca were already to be seen on the horizon, all the winds came jostling each other out of the bag, and a raging storm burst upon their heads. The sails were torn to shreds in an instant. The ships danced like corks on the waves and the gale drove them far from the shores of their native land and into regions where new and perilous adventures awaited them.

Ever since, whenever a sudden violent and destructive wind springs up, men say that Aeolus' bag has been opened.

As we know, Aeolus had six daughters. The most beautiful of these was Alcyone, whom he gave in marriage to Ceyx, king of Trachis.

ALCYONE Alcyone loved her husband dearly, and fear gnawed at her heart each time he sailed too far from shore in search of fish. But Ceyx was such a keen fisherman that nothing she said could hold him back.

But one day, Alcyone felt more than fear — a terrible foreboding that some awful fate would befall her husband, and she begged him not to sail into the open sea.

"I know the currents and the winds," was his reply. "My boat is a sturdy one and there is noone can sail her like me. Besides, the weather is fine and it's too good a day to miss my fishing."

"I don't deny that you're a fine steersman," his wife replied, "and I know you understand the weather and the sea. But there have been times when even my father was caught unawares, even though he rules the winds. I've often heard him say that a raging storm can suddenly blow up in the calmest weather. So I beg you, listen to me for once, and don't put out to sea today."

Perhaps if Ceyx had seen the tears in his wife's eyes he would have done as she wished and not gone fishing. But his pride blinded him to her anguish, obvious though it was.

Such is life. Sometimes we do not even want to know how much pain we cause others, for fear of spoiling our own petty pleasures. And when the time comes to face the consequences, it is too late to be sorry.

The price which Ceyx paid for his selfish pride was a heavy one.

The weather broke without warning when he was far out at sea. A howling gale blew up, whipping the waters into sudden fury. Black clouds scudded across the horizon, hunted by winds which lashed the seas to foam. Within moments, the waves had become mountains — and Ceyx' boat was matchwood.

Alcyone ran desperately down to the shore and, clambering up a tall rock which looked out over the gulf, she anxiously strained her eyes for some sign of her beloved husband until finally she saw his body being carried in on the waves.

Alcyone was distraught. Now, there was nothing she wanted but to give Ceyx one last, passionate, embrace and then join him in death. Impelled by her own despair, she threw herself from the rock into the foaming sea below.

As Alcyone fulfilled her last wish, the gods took pity on her and Ceyx and turned them both into waterbirds. And ever since, they have been called halcyons, or kingfishers. These birds mate for life, and if death carries off the male, his companion tries to end her own life, just as Alcyone did.

THE HALCYONS

Halcyons lay their eggs in the depths of winter; but if the chicks are to hatch the days must be sunny and no chill winds should blow. It is said that ever since Alcyone's time Aeolus has kept the winds in check at midwinter, to allow his daughter, and all other kingfishers, to raise their young in safety. It is a period of gentle and springlike weather in the heart of a bitter season and, even now, we call it "the halcyon days".

DAEDALUS AND ICARUS

From time immemorial man has longed to soar into the sky, but in the distant days which we are talking of it seemed impossible that this bold dream would ever come true.

And yet, mythology tells us that there was a man who not only believed in human flight but actually achieved it.

His name was Daedalus, and with him flew Icarus, his son.

How this came to happen is a story in itself. And the tale begins in Athens, city of wisdom and beauty.

Beneath the Acropolis, near the ancient market place, there were many workshops and studios in those days. In them worked a host of sculptors, painters and other kinds of artists. Outstanding among them was Daedalus, an artist and craftsman of consummate skill descended from the line of Erechtheus.

It is said that the statues Daedalus made were so lifelike that they seemed about to open their lips and speak. His paintings were equally true to life. Yet in spite of this, Daedalus was best known as an architect and inventor. His buildings made the lovely city of Athens fairer still, while among his inventions are counted the geometric compass, the drill, the axe and masts and sails for ships, all of which were significant discoveries for their time.

The people of Athens were so awed by Daedalus' achievements that they said he was taught and helped by Athena herself, goddess of wisdom and the fine arts.

But there were some who envied his talents and wished him ill. For while

great men gather many friends around them, they also make enemies. And in this case, the enemies were able to do great harm to Athena's pupil, as we shall see.

Daedalus had an assistant in his workshop, his sister Perdika's fifteen-year-old son, Talos. A gifted and hard-working lad, he loved his uncle's work, listened carefully to his advice and became more skilful by the day.

One day, Talos wanted to cut a wooden rod in two, and he decided to use the sharp-toothed jawbone of a snake which he had found not long before. The result was a cut so quick and clean it made him sit down and think seriously. In the end, he took a metal blade and filed teeth out of it, just like those on the snake's jaw he had used. With the tool he had made, he could now cut not merely a stick but a whole tree-trunk. And so the first saw came into the world.

Daedalus was impressed by the boy's achievement and proudly showed everyone the new tool which Talos had invented.

"Look, Perdika," he told his sister next day. "See what a clever tool your son has made! Come and see what we can cut now, with this!" And he showed her how beautifully Talos' saw could cut through wood.

"You should look to your laurels," said Perdika laughingly. "For it seems to me that one day Talos will be more than a match for you!"

"That is what I hope for and what I am working towards," replied Daedalus gravely.

But Talos was not destined to go any further along the road to fame.

One day, uncle and nephew were walking on the Acropolis. They were

**THE DEATH
OF TALUS**

picking their way along the rim of the great rock, admiring the city far below and the plain of Attica beyond when, suddenly, disaster struck. Talos stumbled, missed his footing, and, before Daedalus could reach out to save him, he toppled from the edge and was killed.

This terrible mischance was seized on by Daedalus' enemies, evil and mean-minded men, but at the same time ones who wielded great influence. They succeeded in having him dragged before the courts, where they actually accused him of pushing Talos to his death out of jealousy! Though if the truth were known, it was they who were jealous of Daedalus and afraid of the powers given him by his art.

Knowing they had friends among the judges, the accusers shamelessly demanded the death sentence for Daedalus. They did not achieve this aim, but did succeed in getting him banished from Athens for life, even though countless Athenians knew how dearly the great man had loved his nephew, and not one of them was ignorant of the fact that a true artist is incapable of committing a criminal act.

Thus, one blow fell upon the other. A gifted helper and future artist was lost for ever, and on top of the death of Talos came a heavy and unjust sentence which deprived Daedalus of the right to live and work in the city which had given him birth.

Doubly embittered, the great artist took the path of exile. He made his way down to Piraeus and boarded the first vessel which happened to be leaving port. Where it was bound for, he neither knew nor cared. Not till they

had left harbour did he learn that his ship was sailing eastwards to the islands of the Cyclades, calling at Delos, Naxos and Thera, and finally making its way south to the great island of Crete.

In those days, Crete was ruled by the hard-hearted Minos, son of Zeus by Europa. The Crete of king Minos was the mightiest power in the Mediterranean. Its fleet was the largest in the world and its empire at the height of its glory.

Untold wealth had been gathered into its capital, Cnossus, a city which glittered with gold. Luxurious palaces and temples had been raised, along with a host of other opulent and imposing buildings. For Minos was not a man to hide his wealth. He wanted every stranger who set foot on the island to be dazzled by his riches and power.

Minos prided himself on his achievements, but when he came to visit Athens and looked on its temples and statues, the grace of its public buildings and its other works of art, his pride in the show of wealth which adorned Cnossus evaporated immediately. It was then he realized, for the first time, that even if you have all the money in the world, you can create nothing beautiful with it unless you have the training and the instinct of an artist to guide your hand.

So, during his stay in Athens, whenever a particular work of art caught Minos' fancy, he would ask who had created it. And the answer he received would always be the same: Daedalus.

In this way, Minos learned of the greatest artist and inventive craftsman

13

the world had ever known.

When the great king returned to Crete, overwhelmed by his impressions of Athens, his homeland now seemed poor and mean to him, even if it was swimming in gold and feared by every nation upon earth.

"If I had a Daedalus of my own," he kept telling himself, "I should want nothing more in the world."

IN THE SERVICE OF KING MINOS

Then, one day, when he was sitting wrapped in gloomy thoughts upon his solid gold throne, a courtier came jubilantly into his presence.

"Hail, god-born king of mighty Crete!" the courtier cried. "I bring you news which will banish your gloom this very instant, and bring you great joy!"

"There's been nothing but good news recently," replied the king despondently, "but none so good it could shake off my sadness."

"But this time," insisted the courtier, "I believe you have gained what you desire above all things: Daedalus is in Crete, and seeks to enter your service!"

Minos jumped up. "Daedalus in Crete?" he cried joyfully. "I shall run to welcome him in person!"

And welcome him he did, with royal honours, immediately putting at Daedalus' disposal all the means he required to begin his task of beautifying Crete from the very next day.

Thus Cnossus and the rest of the island began to be adorned with graceful buildings and lovely works of art, and Minos could not praise Daedalus too highly.

Daedalus stayed and worked in Crete for many years. He married Naucrate, a lovely girl from the Cyclades, and she bore him a son, Icarus. But she died when the child was still very young.

From his earliest years Icarus learned to love building, painting and sculpture, and his greatest ambition was to follow in his father's footsteps. When he was coming into manhood he helped in the construction of the labyrinth, the greatest of the works which Daedalus undertook in Crete.

The labyrinth was a building of such complexity, with so many rooms and corridors, that whoever entered it could not find his way out again.

In the innermost part of the labyrinth was imprisoned the Minotaur, a man-eating monster with a human body and the head of a bull. This hideous beast was killed by Theseus, the great hero of Athens. By this action he saved his people from the terrible blood-toll they had long paid to the hard-hearted Minos: seven young men and seven maidens who were brought from Athens every year to be devoured by the Minotaur. Daedalus helped Theseus to overcome the monster, and when the king learned of it his anger was terrible. Overnight, Daedalus found himself a prisoner in the very labyrinth he had created, along with Icarus, his son. Now, the two of them had but one thought in their heads: how to find their way out of the maze and flee from Crete.

"Slavery is hard to bear," said Daedalus, "but ten times harder for an

artist. Yet how can we leave Crete if we can't even find our way out of the labyrinth?"

"Only the birds are free," replied his son. "If we could fly like them, we could escape from here. But, alas, the gods did not give men wings."

A DARING PLAN   "They gave them brains, though, Icarus," replied his father, then suddenly fell silent, wrapped in thought.

"Yes, we have brains," continued Icarus, "but if we had wings, too, how wonderful it would be! We would soar high into the sky, as high as the sun; we would travel like the birds, like the clouds, like the gods themselves!"

But Daedalus was no longer paying any attention to his son's words. He was looking fixedly up into the sky and thinking hard, for a bold idea had come into his head.

He was still sitting, wrapped in thought, when Minos' wife, Pasiphae, came to visit the two prisoners.

Pasiphae was not cast in the same cruel mould as her husband, and it grieved her greatly to see the great artist and his son locked up like common criminals. Knowing the loneliness of imprisonment, she would often come to the labyrinth to console them with her company and her conversation.

As soon as he saw the queen, Daedalus burst out:

"There are many things I can bear, but to see these hands lying idle, bound in slavery, that is more than I can endure!"

16

"Even if I could get you out of here," replied the queen, "you would be recaptured at once." And then she added:

"Today, news came from Athens that Theseus has been crowned king, **PASIPHAE** and your banishment has been lifted."

"At last!" cried Daedalus in joy. "Now I can return to my homeland."

"No, Daedalus," replied the queen. "I told you escape was no easy matter, and from now on it will be even more difficult. When Minos learned that the people of Athens wish you to return he was overcome with rage. He ordered guards to be posted all over Crete, even though you are still safely locked up in the labyrinth. He is so afraid that you will get away that he is having the whole coastline watched, and the ports are being checked with such thoroughness that not even a needle could be slipped out undetected. I still want to help you, but I simply don't know how."

"By bringing us feathers," Daedalus answered. "As many feathers as you can lay your hands on. I want swansdown and eagles' quills, storks' pinions and the plumes from vultures' wings. Bring me feathers, and I shall make us wings of our own."

"But Daedalus, I never heard of such a thing," gasped the queen. "How do you know it will work?"

"Bring us the feathers I asked for, if you really want to help," was Daedalus' reply.

The queen was so impressed by the confidence and determination in his voice that she decided to do as she was asked. If anyone had the ingenuity and skill to carry off such a feat, it was Daedalus.

The very next day, Pasiphae began to supply them with feathers, careful to bring them in little by little, in quantities small enough to hide.

Daedalus set to work immediately. With great skill and artistry he fitted them all together, using wax to hold each feather in place. The work was delicate and needed both time and patience, but within a few days the wings had taken shape.

THE PREPARATIONS ARE MADE

There were four of them, like a bird's wings in every respect, but very much larger, and so beautifully made that even the gods would have envied them.

Using leather straps, Daedalus fastened one pair onto Icarus' arms and shoulders, and then he put on his own.

The time to test the wings had come. Beating his arms up and down, Daedalus rose effortlessly into the air. Icarus did the same, and his wings, too, bore him upwards. All was ready!

Before they set off, Daedalus looked his son in the eyes and said:

"Icarus, my child, the journey we are about to make is not an easy one. We have a long way to go, but we shall reach our destination safely if we take care. We must not fly too low, in case the waves soak the feathers, but we must not soar too high, either, for then the sun may melt the wax which holds our wings together. We must travel slowly and steadily, like storks, and then we can be sure of a safe and pleasant flight."

"When shall we reach Athens, father?" asked the young man.

"I do not know, my son," replied Daedalus. "I have thought long and hard about this, and I fear that we should not go there. I am afraid that if we do,

Minos will declare war at once — not only to bring us back to Crete, but to punish Athens for harbouring us. We must not allow bloodshed and destruction to fall upon our city on our account."

"I shall be following you, father, and we shall go wherever you decide."

"That is how it must be, my son," replied Daedalus. "And now the great moment has come — a moment mankind may never forget. Follow me, and remember my advice." And with these words he lifted his great wings and soared into the sky with Icarus close behind.

Moments later they passed over the palace of king Minos, where the anxious Pasiphae had been watching on the great terrace since early morning. Just as they came over, Minos walked out in search of his wife and his eyes beheld a sight beyond belief.

"Pasiphae!" he cried. "Pasiphae! I have never seen such a thing. Two gods flying in the sky!"

"Gods indeed," replied Pasiphae and turned her face aside so that he should not see the tears which filled her eyes.

Daedalus and Icarus flew surely and steadily onwards. Soon they were looking down on the first of the Cyclades, an island shaped like a half moon. This was Thera, or all that was left of it after the great volcanic eruption which had engulfed the island's centre.

Flying northwards, they came to Naxos, the island of Dionysus, and then Delos, with its great temple of Apollo. At last, open sea stretched out beneath them once more.

Icarus was delighted with his new wings and swooped and soared as he

**LIKE
WINGED GODS**

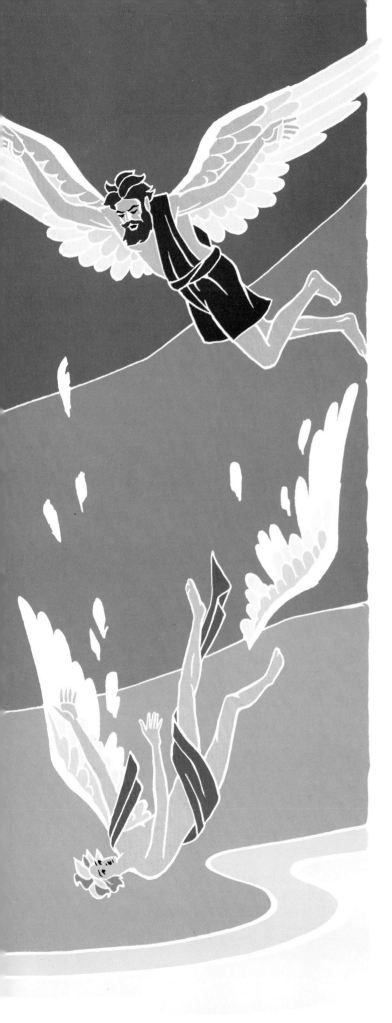

ICARUS FALLS

flew. Harmless games enough they seemed, but Daedalus was worried, and cried out:

"Steady there, Icarus!"

"Don't worry, father," the boy shouted back, "there's no danger."

"There is, my boy, there is. Be careful. We're on a journey, not playing games!"

But unfortunately, Icarus thought he knew everything, and would not listen to his father's advice. That is how Phaethon came to a sad end, and that is how Icarus, too, was destined to die. So it has been for thousands of years, and so it will always be. Yet mankind needs courage, and youth cannot be blamed if it has more daring than its elders.

And Icarus was nothing if not daring. The higher he went, the more his spirits rose. The sun drew him like a magnet, and his father's warning flew right out of his mind.

When Daedalus next turned his head to check that all was well with Icarus, there was no sign of the boy. Close to panic, he scanned the skies from horizon to horizon, till finally he made out a tiny dot, rapidly approaching the sun's bright disc.

"Icarus!" he shouted despairingly. "Icarus, come back!" But in spite of the urgency of Daedalus' voice, his words were lost in the boundless expanses of the sky and never reached his son's ears.

And soon the very thing happened which Daedalus had feared. The sun melted the wax and the feathers were scattered in the air. Soon there was not a single feather left, and Icarus fell like a stone from the heights. With frantic wingbeats, Daedalus made a desperate effort to catch him, but it was all in vain, and the daring young man found a watery grave in the arms of the blue sea far below.

On labouring wings Daedalus carried the body of his son to the nearest island, and there he buried him. Ever since, the island has been called Icaria and the sea around it, the Icarian sea, and all over the world the name of Icarus is remembered whenever men wish to honour those who gave their lives to make the dream of flight come true.

Shattered by the death of his son, Daedalus now had but one wish: to put the greatest distance possible between himself and the place where the boy had fallen. And so he flew westwards, on and on, until he reached Sicily.

When he at last made landfall, his first act was to destroy the wings which had cost Icarus his life. Then he made his way to the court of king Cocalus and offered his services in return for royal protection.

Cocalus received Daedalus gladly and entrusted a number of important projects to him including, it is said, the mighty walls of Acragantus in southern Sicily.

Meanwhile, Minos had not been sitting with folded hands. As soon as he learned of Daedalus' escape, he set out with a mighty fleet to find the master craftsman and bring him back to Crete.

Minos did not expect any help in his task. Wherever Daedalus had gone, the local people would want to keep him for themselves. And so the king of Crete employed a cunning trick. He did not reveal that he was searching for Daedalus, but took with him a conch shell, a gift from the sea god, Triton. This shell had a small hole at its pointed end, and, by blowing through it, Triton could raise storms and gales.

Everywhere he went, Minos would show people the shell and ask if anyone could pass a thread through its open mouth, round the spirals of the interior and out of the hole. And, of course, he promised a rich reward to the first man who could solve the problem.

Minos went all over the world without finding a single person who could pass a thread through the shell, until at last he came to Sicily and gave it to king Cocalus. He accepted the challenge and took the shell to Daedalus, and the cunning inventor, having smeared a little honey round the narrow opening at its tip, placed an ant in the broad lip of the shell, with a fine thread tied to its leg. Drawn by the sweet scent of the honey, the ant made its way down the spirals of the interior drawing the thread behind it till it reached the small hole at the other end. Bursting with pride, Cocalus bore the threaded shell back to king Minos.

As soon as he set eyes on it, Minos knew whose work this was. There was no one in the world could find the answer to such a problem except the man he had been searching for so long.

"This is the work of Daedalus!" he shouted joyfully. "Bring him here immediately, for he returns to Crete with me!"

Now Cocalus had no wish at all to deliver Daedalus into the hands of this Cretan tyrant, but on the other hand he had a healthy respect for Minos' evil temper and the huge army that lay on board his ships. He knew that if he dared refuse, the ruler of Crete would bring him and his kingdom to ruin.

And so he promised to release Daedalus, and meanwhile invited Minos to enjoy the hospitality of his palace. By now, all Sicily was up in arms, for not a man on the island wanted Daedalus to fall into the cruel king's hands.

"We would rather go down fighting than betray a man who sought our protection," they cried, "especially one who has done so many wonderful things for us."

When Cocalus saw their mood, he took his closest advisers aside to find some means of ridding themselves of Minos. And in the end they found a way. While he was taking a bath, they poured two cauldrons of boiling water on his body, scalding him to death. And so the Cretan forces would not attack, they claimed it had all been an accident.

Such was the inglorious end of the feared and mighty king of Crete.

Yet after his death Minos became one of the judges of the shades in Hades, as we saw in an earlier book. He may have been cruel and unjust on earth but he was, after all, a son of Zeus and mankind had to learn to bow to the will of the gods, just or unjust as it might be.

HOME AT LAST After Minos died, Daedalus returned at last to Athens where he spent the rest of his days, working and teaching true art to younger men to the very last. Towards the end of his life, he founded the school which bore his name. It survived for hundreds of years and the many great artists that it bred were all called Daedalides

PELOPS AND OENOMAUS

Whoever goes to Olympia today and visits its museum will certainly stand in awe before the statues which once adorned the two pediments of the temple of Zeus. The one which decorated the eastern end shows the chariot race between Pelops and Oenomaus, while the western one depicts the battle between the Centaurs and the Lapiths.

If only because they are portrayed in such great works of art, these two myths deserve to be retold.

But before we begin the myth of Oenomaus and Pelops, we must tell the story of the latter's father, Tantalus.

TANTALUS

In Phrygia, in Asia Minor, beneath the sacred mountain Tmolus, where Midas had once been king, Tantalus, son of Zeus by the oceanid Pluto, was now upon the throne.

Tantalus had all that a ruler could wish for. His ploughlands were fertile and gave bountiful crops. His lush meadows were filled with grazing flocks led by curly-horned rams, while riders on proud horses drove great herds of cattle to other pastures. Every day, rich gifts reached the court of Tantalus, the offerings of chiefs who acknowledged his dominion. And besides all this wealth he had the gold washed down from the mountains by the Pactolus, the richest gold-bearing river in the world.

As if all this were not enough, Tantalus enjoyed a closer friendship with the gods than any other man on earth. They would often come from Olympus to eat, drink and make merry with him in his golden palaces, and at other times they would invite him to their symposia on Olympus to drink nectar and ambrosia with the gods.

Zeus was so fond of his son that he would even ask him to attend their councils and join with the Olympians in taking those great decisions which determined the fate of mankind.

But the love shown to him by Zeus and the other gods filled Tantalus with such pride that he began to consider himself their superior. Little by little, his respect for them diminished. He began to take nectar and ambrosia from Olympus to toast his friends on earth, and he revealed the secrets of the gods to mortal men to show the world what a splendid fellow he was. Zeus warned him that if he wished to keep his friendship with the Olympians he must be more careful, but Tantalus replied in an insolent and haughty tone:

PRIDE COMES BEFORE A FALL

"I shall do whatever I please. I am a mighty ruler in my own right, and I accept advice from no one."

Zeus frowned his disapproval, but he loved his son so much that he let his pride go unpunished.

The only result of this was an even worse act of impiety on Tantalus' part: he swore a false oath to the gods, solemnly declaring he had no idea what had become of their beloved golden dog of Crete, whereas the truth was that he not only knew the whereabouts of their favourite animal, but had hidden it himself!

Until that moment, no god had ever lied on oath, and every mortal who had done so had paid the penalty. Zeus was enraged when he heard what his son had done. Yet once again his fatherly love overcame his harsher feelings and Tantalus went unpunished.

Instead of being grateful for the mercy Zeus had shown him, Tantalus took the gods' inaction for a sign of weakness. Blinded by his high opinion of himself, he came to believe that the only real proof of power was to commit the most hideous crime imaginable without suffering any of its evil consequences.

Once this sick belief had planted itself in his head, Tantalus began to

THE TORTURES OF TANTALUS

rack his brain for the cruellest and most horrible act a man could dream of. And, unfortunately, he was not long in finding it: he decided to butcher his own son and serve him up to the gods at a banquet. His aim was not only to humiliate them, but to show the world that the Olympians were not the all-knowing creatures they liked mankind to think them, if they could not even tell what they were eating!

So Tantalus invited the gods to his palace and served them the vilest meal the world had ever known.

But there was no deceiving the immortals: they knew at once what had been set before them and refused to touch the meat. Now, all eyes turned on Zeus. The countenance of the ruler of gods and men had blackened with fearsome rage. Thunder and lightning shook the earth. A crime such as this could never go unpunished and, with a look of loathing, Zeus hurled his son into the dark kingdom of Hades to suffer eternal torture.

Tantalus was condemned to stand in a pool of crystal-clear water. He was soon afflicted by thirst and wished to drink, but as soon as he leaned forward to do so the water disappeared, leaving only parched, dry earth where it had been. Immediately he returned to an upright position, the water came flooding back waist-high. Again and again Tantalus tried to quench his thirst, but he could not even catch a single drop to wet his cracked and burning lips. He was condemned to the torture of eternal thirst. But this was not all. Over his head hung branches laden with ripe and luscious fruit, and Tantalus was torn by the most terrible pangs of hunger. He stretched up a hand to pluck a fruit and ease the pain which clutched at his entrails, but as he did so the branches rose beyond his grasp. Time and again he reached upwards, but each time he reached in vain. He was condemned to the torture of eternal hunger. And as if these unbearable punishments were not enough, a third was added to them: a huge rock hung teetering above Tantalus' head, threatening to fall at any moment and crush him beneath its weight. Every time it swayed or creaked, Tantalus was seized with terror. Yet the rock never fell upon him, and so he was condemned to the torture of eternal fear.

TANTALUS' SON IS BROUGHT BACK TO LIFE

When Zeus saw that the miserable king of Phrygia was well punished for his horrible deed, he called Hermes and ordered him to gather up all the pieces of Tantalus' son from the table, to wash them well and then to fit together once again the young man who had been so cruelly slaughtered. Hermes obeyed his father's orders with great care and skill, but when he had finished there was a piece still missing from the shoulder. It had been eaten by Demeter, who had lost her daughter, Persephone, and was too upset to realize what was on her plate. However, Hephaestus replaced the missing part with cunningly worked ivory and finally Zeus breathed life into the body. The young man who had been saved was named Pelops, and he would always have an ivory patch on his shoulder. For that reason they still say that anyone who has a white mark on any part of the body is a descendant of his.

Pelops succeeded to his father's throne, but he did not rule for long. He was defeated in battle by the king of Troy and obliged to flee his kingdom.

With him he took his sister, Niobe, of whom we shall tell in the next book, and as much of his father's gold as he could carry. Then, together with a few faithful friends, he made his way westwards into Greece.

His wanderings finally brought him to Pisa, a city near Olympia ruled by king Oenomaus.

Oenomaus had a beautiful daughter, Hippodameia, but he did not wish to find a husband for her because the oracle had warned him that he was destined to be killed by the man she married. To forestall this fate, Oenomaus decided to kill every man who asked him for her hand, and he warned all prospective suitors that he would only give away his daughter if

one of them could beat him in a chariot race. Whoever lost would die on the end of Oenomaus' lance.

The contest was one-sided: the king was always as sure of victory as his opponents were of death, for his horses were swifter than the wild north wind and he was the finest charioteer in the whole of Greece.

In spite of this, Hippodameia's beauty had already drawn thirteen suitors to accept the challenge and pit their skills against the king of Pisa. All of them had been defeated and had met their end at the point of his cruel lance.

And now Pelops decided to face Oenomaus, for he, too, had fallen under the spell of Hippodameia's charms.

Hippodameia loved Pelops and she begged him not to add his name to the long list of fallen heroes.

"His horses are the swiftest in the world and there is not a charioteer in Greece can match him. I would rather you went away and never saw me again than learn that you had sacrificed your life for me."

"I shall not lose my life," replied Pelops, "but Oenomaus will lose a daughter. My horses were a gift from Poseidon himself and they are as swift as the wind. The gods are on my side, and they will help me to win."

And so Pelops appeared before Oenomaus, asked his daughter's hand in marriage and declared himself ready for the chariot race.

"Very well," was the king's answer. "Since you place no value on your young life, then neither shall I. I shall do you the same favour I have always done the others and let you set off an hour before me, but as soon as my

chariot overtakes yours, I shall kill you."

Pelops, however, had Hermes on his side.

"Are we going to let him die now, when we went to so much trouble to undo his father's murderous work?" he asked.

Exactly the same thought had been running through Zeus' mind, so with his father's blessing Hermes hastened to find his son Myrtilus, who was the king of Pisa's chief charioteer.

"Listen, Myrtilus," said Hermes. "This time I want Oenomaus to be killed and not his opponent. I want you to see to it that something goes wrong with your master's chariot during the race."

Now Myrtilus lacked none of his wily father's cunning, and it did not take him long to work out what to do.

That night, he went to Oenomaus' chariot, took out the locking pin which held the off-side wheel to the axle and replaced it with another, made of wax.

The contest was to begin next morning. They would set off from the temple of Zeus at Olympia and race eastwards for the Isthmus of Corinth, in an attempt to reach the temple of Poseidon there by dusk.

As usual, Oenomaus gave his opponent an hour's start while he went to sacrifice to Zeus. By the time the sacrifice had been made Pelops was well ahead, but Oenomaus jumped into his chariot and shot off like a bolt of lightning. However, Tantalus' son had swift horses too and so the king of Pisa rode on for some hours without seeing any sign of him. Oenomaus began to feel anxious and whipped his horses up to a faster pace. It was the first time he had come so far without overtaking his opponent. Finally he made out Pelops' chariot way ahead in the distance. The sight gave Oenomaus renewed confidence and his horses surged forward as if filled

with new strength. The gap between them narrowed steadily. Pelops turned his head and saw the fearsome Oenomaus advancing on him like a storm-front. A desperate race began. Pelops' horses thundered wildly forwards, as if they knew some dreadful enemy was descending upon them. Oenomaus strained to close the distance, but with a superhuman effort Pelops urged his horses into an even faster gallop. The two opponents sped onwards, their hearts in their mouths, knowing only too well that this was a race between life and death. Oenomaus made another great effort, lashing his horses furiously, and little by little he began to gain ground. Pelops' horses could go no faster and the gap was closing quicker. Nothing could hold Oenomaus now. His feet beat a frenzied rhythm on the chariot floor and his deadly javelin quivered in his hand. A savage joy shone in his face as he saw the moment of victory and death draw near. The end of the race was in sight: away in the distance, the temple of Poseidon could just be made out. Oenomaus came on faster still. Pelops struggled hopelessly to pull ahead, but his horses had given the last ounce of their strength. "O, gods!" he cried. "Why abandon me now, when you saved me from my father's wrath!" But it seemed that the gods had indeed forgotten him, for the wax pin still held as firm as iron and Oenomaus surged forward like a hurricane, his wheels beating a wild tattoo on the stony track. The moment he was waiting for had come. With a hair-raising cry he flexed his arm to plunge his deadly lance in Pelops' back, when suddenly his right wheel flew into the air, the royal chariot overturned and Oenomaus was dragged headlong over the stones to a horrible death. That was the end of the bloodthirsty king of Pisa, and that, too, was the end of the race. Thanks to Myrtilus, Pelops was declared the victor, married the lovely Hippodameia and became the ruler of Oenomaus' kingdom.

**A RACE
TO THE DEATH**

But as you will have noticed, there are few happy endings in the stories we have to tell. For all their magical inventiveness, myths are not fairy tales where "they all lived happily ever after," and the story of Pelops is no exception to the rule.

When he learned it was Hermes himself who had saved him, the new king of Pisa built a temple in his honour, the first that had ever been raised in the god's name in the whole world. He also summoned Myrtilus to receive his reward.

PELOPS TRICKS MYRTILUS

"Ask me for whatever you wish, and I shall give it to you," Pelops announced, without asking himself what Myrtilus might now demand. And it was an unwelcome answer that Hermes' son had ready for him: he wanted half Pelops' new kingdom, neither more nor less.

The thought of handing over such a prize was a painful one. All night long Pelops dwelt on it, and in the morning he went in search of Myrtilus and took him out into the country on the pretext of pacing out the boundaries of the young charioteer's share of the land. But instead of this, he led him to the summit of a high cliff and with a sudden push sent him tumbling into the foaming seas below.

As he fell to his death, Myrtilus laid a curse on Pelops and all his descendants. The son of Tantalus begged Hermes to protect him from the evil spell, but though the god had saved him twice before, this time Pelops begged in vain. Hermes turned a deaf ear, for he had killed not only his son but the man who had helped to save his life. Myrtilus' curse took hold: Pelops, his children and his children's children suffered great misfortunes, committed foul crimes and were punished harshly by the gods. Yet for all this the name of Pelops was not forgotten. The land to which he had come was given his name, and has been known as the Peloponnese ever since.

This is the tragic story told in marble on the eastern pediment of the temple of Zeus at Olympia. The other brings the tale of the Lapiths and the Centaurs to life.

The Lapiths were a race who lived in Thessaly. One of their kings was Ixion, whom we have spoken of in an earlier book. There, we also learned how the first Centaur was born. Most people say the Centaurs were the descendants of Ixion and Nephele. They were strange creatures, half horse and half man, and wild, too, with a few exceptions such as the wise Centaur, Cheiron, who was also immortal. Many mythical figures came to him to be taught, even gods, like Asclepius, who learned medicine at his side.

The Centaurs were neighbours of the Lapiths. They lived on Mount Pelion, and, until the time of this story, there had been no quarrels between them.

The king of the Lapiths was now the hero Peirithous. He was about to celebrate his wedding to the lovely Deidameia and had announced a great feast, with heroes from all over Greece as his guests. As the Centaurs were descended from a Lapith king he invited them to the celebrations, too, along with their leader, Eurytion, and offered them hospitality in a cave near his palace.

Peirithous' servants set tables in the cave and loaded them with rich food and great flagons of strong wine. The centaurs, however, not knowing such liquor should be mixed with water, swallowed it neat and were soon roaring drunk.

In his cups, Eurytion was seized by an irresistible urge. With a clatter of hooves he galloped out of the cave, burst into the great banqueting hall of the palace and tried to seize Peirithous' lovely bride.

31

Livid with rage at this insult, which showed no more respect for him than for his bride, Peirithous drew his sword and launched himself at Eurytion. The other guests followed suit, and the leader of the Centaurs fled back to the cave, his face streaming blood.

"Look what Peirithous has done to me!" he cried. "Come on, let's go back and carry off their wives!"

THE BATTLE WITH THE CENTAURS

These words were all the excuse the drunken Centaurs needed to storm into the palace and throw themselves on the Lapith women.

The Lapiths drew their swords once more, and a savage battle now began. The Centaurs armed themselves with chairs and tripods, broken table legs and whatever else in the palace they could lay their hands on. Soon the walls echoed with the dreadful din of their fighting. The Lapiths defended their women with great heroism, but even so, some of the Centaurs managed to snatch up Lapith girls and carry them off, at which the others galloped out after them. Peirithous came running in pursuit, his countrymen and the other heroes close behind, and the battle was resumed in the open air as fiercely as before. The Centaurs used their immense strength to heave huge boulders at the heroes and beat at them with wooden clubs, but at the critical moment Peirithous' good friend Theseus, the mighty hero of Athens, came to the Lapiths' aid. Eurytion was the first to fall beneath his blows, and at this the Lapiths took courage, and, led by the Athenian champion, they fell on the Centaurs with renewed strength. The battle became a bloodbath and only a handful of Centaurs managed to escape by fleeing to the mountains. But not even these lived long. Within a few years they all met their deaths, pierced by the deadly arrows of Heracles, whom they had tried to kill.

And so the forests and the mountains were freed from the wild and savage Centaurs. Not even Cheiron escaped, though Heracles had not wished to harm him. Mortally wounded by a stray arrow, yet still immortal, the wise Centaur suffered all the pangs of death for many years, until he could endure no longer and begged Zeus to let him die and so release him from eternal agony.

SOME ANSWERS TO POSSIBLE QUERIES

To those of our readers, young or old, whose reading of this mythology series may have prompted certain questions, we would like to say the following:

It is possible that you may have read the same myth elsewhere and noticed significant differences. This does not necessarily mean that one version is right and the other wrong. In their retelling, myths came to differ widely from place to place and from age to age and as a result several versions are now extant. In this work, we decided to give one version only, choosing either that most widely accepted, or the one we felt to have the most value. Working by the same criteria we have often added materials taken from other sources to round out a myth.

Another frequent cause of bewilderment are the contradictions generally encountered in mythology. For example, in one myth Zeus may be depicted as kind and fair, and in another tyrannical and unjust. Even Homer does much the same thing in the Iliad. At one point he has Thersites, a common soldier, lashing Agamemnon himself with the tongue of truth, while at another we see him crying like a child beneath the blows of Odysseus' gilded sceptre. These apparent contradictions must be accepted at face value, for it must not be forgotten that while sceptred monarchs had the right to command, the story-teller's lyre was in the hands of the common people, and clashes were inevitable. It is significant that while rulers are depicted as being the equals of Ares in power and daring, the singer-poets did not create a single myth in which the god of war emerges victorious, but many in which he suffers defeat and humiliation.

As for the illustrations, we believe that a picture should speak for itself. Nevertheless, we should like to say a few words about them.

We had to choose between two schools of thought. According to the one —and this is a line taken by many illustrators— we would have been obliged to remain faithful to the classical originals, chiefly vase-paintings, working in two dimensions, without perspective and with sparing use of colour. The other approach dictated that we use a modern style, and this we have preferred — but with one important prerequisite: that the picture, like the text, must itself be mythology. Thus, while keeping to the classical line, we have added a few elements of perspective where this seemed absolutely necessary. In one respect, however, we felt that we must have absolute freedom, and that was in the colouring. In our opinion, it was precisely the bright colours we have used which would give our work the fairytale air which the myths have to the modern reader's eye. For the ancients, in contrast, mythology was religion. For them the gods were real and not mythical beings. To us mythology is something else — a collection of wise and charming stories which shine like a bright fabric of the imagination from out of the depths of the centuries. It is for this reason that we have tried to illustrate this series with colour alone, or rather, by weaving harmonious contrasts of colour, but never forgetting that our theme is Greek mythology.